THE WHALE COMEDIAN

BY **MARTIN NELSON** **BURTON** **JORDAN**

ILLUSTRATED BY **CHARLES**

For Arden:
Never give up
on your dreams!

August 2011

LONDON TOWN PRESS

For Patrick—the original whale comedian—M.N.B.

For Charlie and Maggie—C.J.

Printed in Hong Kong by South China Printing Co. (1988) Ltd.
Book design by Christy Hale.

Publisher's Cataloging in Publication Data
Burton, Martin Nelson
The whale comedian / by Martin Nelson Burton;
illustrated by Charles Jordan.—1st ed.
p. cm.
Summary: A young boy named Finston
succeeds in becoming a comedian who can make whales
spit water, which is their way of laughing.
1. Whales—Juvenile fiction.   2. Comedians—Juvenile fiction.
3. Marine parks and reserves—Juvenile fiction.   I. Jordan, Charles.   II. Title.
PZ7.B9536Wh 1999   [E] QBI99-9   LCCN: 98-96954   ISBN: 0-9666490-8-7

10   9   8   7   6   5   4   3   2

whale comedian (wāl kuh-mē' dē-un) *n. A person who tells jokes and funny stories to whales. When whales like what they hear, they don't laugh, like people do. They spit water. A good whale comedian will come out very, very wet by the end of the act.*

Everyone agreed that Finston was the most serious boy they had ever met. He certainly looked serious.

But inside, Finston knew that he was really very funny. He wanted to be a whale comedian.

Finston would do anything to make a whale happy. He liked to gurgle funny noises to his toy killer whale. The little whale always seemed very pleased.

As he got older, Finston believed that he could make other whales happy, too.

So one day, he set off, wherever there were whales, to tell them jokes and make them forget their troubles.

He sailed onto the high seas and called out
jokes whenever he saw whales.

"... So she says, 'Oh Harold!
I told you to bring me fish and
chips, not fish and **ships**!'"

This could be dangerous. It was not always easy to tell the difference between a wild whale that was enjoying a joke and one that did not like it at all.

And it was hard even to find whales. Sometimes, he would have to make up jokes just for dolphins. He would trip and fall right on top of his audience.

Then he'd get out and say, *"I did that on **porpoise**!"*
The dolphins had usually heard that one before.

Finston decided it might be safer instead to visit tame animals. He traveled to marine amusement parks, where whales perform.

He would explain to the trainers what he could do for the whales.

That clearly made a lot of **people** laugh,
but nobody ever gave him a chance to try
his act on the whales.

Finston never gave up. He came back to
his favorite park to watch the killer whale
show. The whales looked very tired.

After the performance, Finston walked right up to the glass tank and waited for a whale to swim by. When one came close, Finston started telling his best jokes.

"I was going to tell you the one about the whale that ate its trainer, but I decided it would be **in bad taste!**"

But no matter how loud he shouted or how hard he tried, the whale didn't spit water. It paid no attention at all. The whale just swam sadly underwater, around and around and around.

"Do you know why a mother whale sees
all the bad things her children do?
...Because she has **eyes in the
back of her head!**"

"Why don't whales eat sushi?
...The chopsticks keep getting stuck
between their teeth!"

"But seriously, I didn't
come here to **make waves!**"

"Hello! Hello!
Is this thing on?"

Finally, Finston got an idea. He leaned close to the glass and stuck out his tongue.

The whale suddenly stopped and looked at him.

He made another silly face. The whale
swam nearer.

At last the whale could not stand it any longer. It leaped up high into the air, splattered Finston with a shower of water, and flopped back down with a huge splash that soaked Finston from head to toe.

The trainers rushed over to see what had happened. The whale was twirling around in delight. When they saw how happy Finston had made the tired whale, they knew right then that they needed a whale comedian.

Finston's fame soon spread, and before long
he was invited to marine parks all over the world.
Everywhere he went, whales began to perform
better than ever.

Now, the whales always wait politcly until he has finished his jokes. Thcn Finston will start dancing and making faces, and the real fun will begin.

Of course, when he goes back to school, he still sits down quietly and puts on a serious face. But now, Finston thinks about all the happy whales. And that's when Finston smiles.